ANDERS and the VOLCANO

Gregory Mackay

ALLEN&UNWIN
SYDNEY • MELBOURNE • AUCKLAND • LONDON

For the inquisitive

First published in 2016

Allen & Unwin
83 Alexander Street
Crows Nest NSW 2065
Australia
Phone: (61 2) 8425 0100
Email: info@allenandunwin.com
Web: www.allenandunwin.com

A Cataloguing-in-Publication entry is available
from the National Library of Australia
www.trove.nla.gov.au

ISBN 978 1 76029 003 0

Cover and text design by Gregory Mackay and Sandra Nobes
This book was printed in May 2016 at McPherson's Printing Group Australia
www.mcphersonsprinting.com.au

1 3 5 7 9 10 8 6 4 2

anderscomics.com

The paper in this book is FSC® certified. FSC® promotes environmentally responsible, socially beneficial and economically viable management of the world's forests.

Hello, I'm Anders and these are my friends Bernie and Eden. The holidays are almost here again and I can't wait to see what happens!

Mount Tremble
National Park
N
W
E
S

Chapter 1

RUMPLE
SCHOOL
'Forever
Clever'

I can't believe the holidays are almost here, Bernie.

I know. It's the last day of school already.

I'm so excited!

What do you have planned?

Um...

...I don't know.

We're going camping for some of the time.

It's going to be ace!

Oh.

Will you go away?
Dad's working.
So I don't think so.
How about I ask Mum and Dad if you can come too?
?
Really?
Do you think they'd let me?
I think so!
Oh wow, this is great!
I'll ask Dad tonight.
Hey, that's the bell.
DING DING
Let's go!

I wonder what holiday homework we'll get this time?
Maybe it'll be a drawing or something.
No, it'll probably be a diorama project.
What would you know, Terry?
Yeah, Terry.
Pfft!
Then.
okay, class, the homework for the break will be a diorama project.
You'll need to build a model of something you see on your study break.

Later.
Good guess, Terry.
Oh, I just asked earlier on.
That's clever.
Well, have a good holiday, Terry.
Okay, bye Anders. Bye, Bernie.
Bye!
Skip should be here soon.
Look, there he is.

Hi, Skip.
SKIP
Can you come over tomorrow, Bernie?
That way we can talk about going on holidays.
Okay!
Great, see you then.
C'mon, Skip.
HOP
SKIP

We're almost there, Skip.
Home again.
Hi, Anders.
Hello!

How was school today?
It was okay.
Miss gave us homework again.
I have to make a diorama.
That sounds fun.
Dad's right, Anders, you love building models.
Oh, yeah.
You'll need to think of a good idea.
Okay!
And remember not to leave it to the last minute!

Later.
Z Z Z Z Z Z

Dad, where are we going for our holiday?

Well, we're going to Mount Tremble.

What's that?

Mount Tremble is an extinct volcano.

There's a big lake there and a camping village.

We're going to stop over at Cape Capsize on the way and stay the night.

Then we'll drive to Mount Tremble.

Will it take long to get there?

No, it'll be fun.

You can read about it in this book.

Wow!

MOUNT TREMBLE
NATIONAL PARK
CAMP CANVAS
LAKE DEPTHCHARGE

Chapter 2

The next day.
Dad, do you know what?
What?
I love cereal!
Knock
Knock
I'll get it!
Hi, Anders.
Oh hi, Bernie. Come on in.

Hey, Mum?
Yes, Anders?
Can Bernie come with us on holidays?
May I?
Ha ha, of course you can, Bernie!
There's plenty of room for everyone!
Yay!
Let's go play!
Come back in time for Whump!

We're going to have a great time at Mount Tremble.
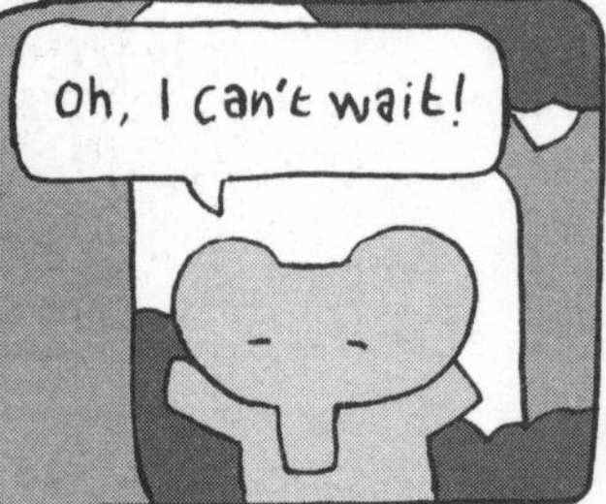
Oh, I can't wait!

I've never been there before.

I've got a book on it, though.

You can borrow it, if you like.

THUMP THUMP THUMP

What was that?

I don't know.

Let's go find out.

Okay!

Look!

I wonder who's up there.

HELLO?

Hello?

Who's there?

Oh, look!
It's Eden.

what're you doing?

I'm working on my tree house.

Come on up and have a look.

This place is amazing, Eden.

Did you build it all by yourself?

I sure did!

Mum helped me with the plans...

...and some of the other stuff.

But I did all the hammering!

There's lots of room for storage.

We already have a cubby, though.

Why did you build this tree house?

Oh, I just wanted my own room.

Hey, look, it's nearly time for Whump!

It is too.
Let's go, Skip.

See you guys there.

WHUMP

Where've you guys been?
I've been here for ages.

Not everyone can fly y'know, Anders!

Soon.

Okay kids, that's all for today.

I'm tired.

Are you going to fly home now, Anders?

No, I think I'll walk home with you guys.

Bye, guys.
See ya.
Bye.

C'mon, Skip.

Chapter 3

Later on, at the cubby house.

I'm bored.

Me, too.

I know, let's dig a pond!

Hey, yeah!

What are you guys doing?

Digging a pond.

How will you fill it up with water?

SPLOOOSH

Where did all the water go?

It got absorbed into the ground!

It's a big MUD PILE!

SQWUDGE

I love the mud pond.
Will there be mud on our holiday, Anders?

Well, it's at a lake, so maybe.
Yeah, we can all go swimming.

But I can't swim.

Um...well, that's okay, I'll be there.
There'll be boats to float on. You'll be just fine!

Oh, I like boats.
Yeah, it's going to be fun.

Later.

Ready, Anders? It's almost time to go.

Where are we going again?

Old Rumple Town!

What's that?

It's a historic adventure town.

C'mon, it'll be fun!

Soon.
Is this really going to be fun, Dad?
!

Wow, Dad!

Let's go!

What's this thing, Dad?

That's a watermill.

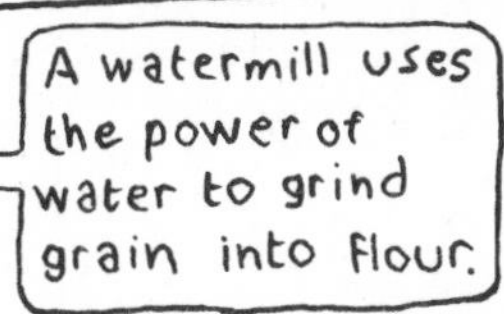
A watermill uses the power of water to grind grain into flour.

Grain
Millstones
Gears

That's cool.

Hey, look over there, Dad!

Funny cars!

They're vintage microcars, Anders.

Ha! Tiny cars!

Hi, Anders.

Hi!

Hey, look Anders, that kid has a little friend like Skip.

Woah!

I'm going to say hi.

Hello, I'm Anders.

I can't believe you've got a grasshopper.

BOUNCE

Wow, Veronica can fly too!
C'mon Skip, let's catch up!
Back soon.
Hop
SKIP

Hey!
Veronica!
I can fly, like you!
Want to be friends?
BOUNCE
Woah!

Bounce must make some kind of shock wave.
Let's go, Skip.
Are you okay, Anders?

Chapter 4

Are you almost ready, Anders?

Almost!

I just have to finish packing.

Ready!

Are we picking up Bernie and Eden?
Sure are.
Look, Mums! There they are!
See you guys there.
Okay, we'll be following you.
Jump in, Eden.
Then.
Have a great time, Bernie. Send me a postcard.
Bye, Dad.

Are you guys alright back there?

YESSS!

Okay then!

Holidays, here we come.

Later that day.
Wake up, Kids. We're at Cape Capsize.
Time for ice-cream.
KIOSK

Well guys, let's spend the rest of the day at the beach...
...then head to the caravan park.
Yay!
Wanna go for a swim, guys?
I can't swim, remember?
That's okay, Bernie, you can paddle. We'll watch you.

I think it's time to head to the caravan park.
Awww, really?
Yes, It's time to go, guys. Let's pack up.
Soon.

Right kids, this caravan is yours tonight.

You mean we get our own caravan?!

That's right.

Ha ha ha.

Look! We get our own bunks.

Mine's the best. It has a reading light.

Time for dinner, you guys.

Later that night.

Hey guys, guess what?

What?

I met another kid who can fly with a beetle.

What?!

No way!

I did!
She was a kid called Veronica.

She has a grasshopper called Bounce.

Was Bounce as fast as you and Skip?

Faster!

Bounce has some kind of power boost.

Woah.

Yeah.

Do you know what that means?

If we're lucky, we might find beetles too, Bernie.

Um... I might be afraid of flying.

Chapter 5

When do we get to the volcano?

LOOKOUT

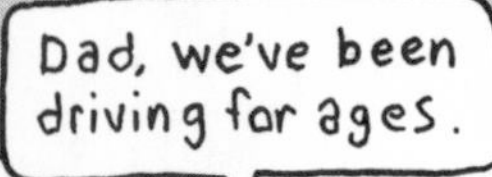
Dad, we've been driving for ages.

Can Skip and I go flying?

Alright, Anders. Five minutes.

Don't go far.
I won't. I'll be right back. Ready, Skip?

Soon.
One hour later.
WELCOME
CAMP CANVAS
MOUNT TREMBLE
NATIONAL PARK

Wake up, guys.
We're here!

And here's our camp site.

You kids have a cabin to share. We have the cabin next door.

Wow, check it out.

This is great, Eden!

Actually, I brought a tent to pitch.

Do you need a hand?

No, I'll be fine.

Nice tent, Eden.

Thanks.

You can play in the cabin anytime you like.

Thanks, guys.

Hey, look.

I have a map of the camp.

CAMP CANVAS
MT TREMBLE
Ranger station
Gate
Office
Cabins
Laundry
Lake Depthcharge
Cabins
Kiosk

The General
Duckboard forest
Games room
Huts
mess hall
To the volcano

Later on.
I love our bunk beds.
Yeah, they're cool.
Let's go check out the games room.
Yeah!

DRIVE AT
WALKING
PACE

KIOSK

Let's get an ice-cream!

HONK HONK

No way! It's that kid who can fly too!

Is she your friend?

I don't know.

KIOSK
1908
Look, postcards.
I'm going to write a postcard to Dad now.

Dear Dad,
I really like
camp and
miss you heaps
BERnie
Mount Tremble
National park.
10c ROYAL
SNAIL
Dad
10 Branch Ave
Rumple
1001
mount Tremble

Chapter 6

What're you guys up to today?

Um...

...we were just going to walk around checking things out.

Great! Don't forget to take a map.

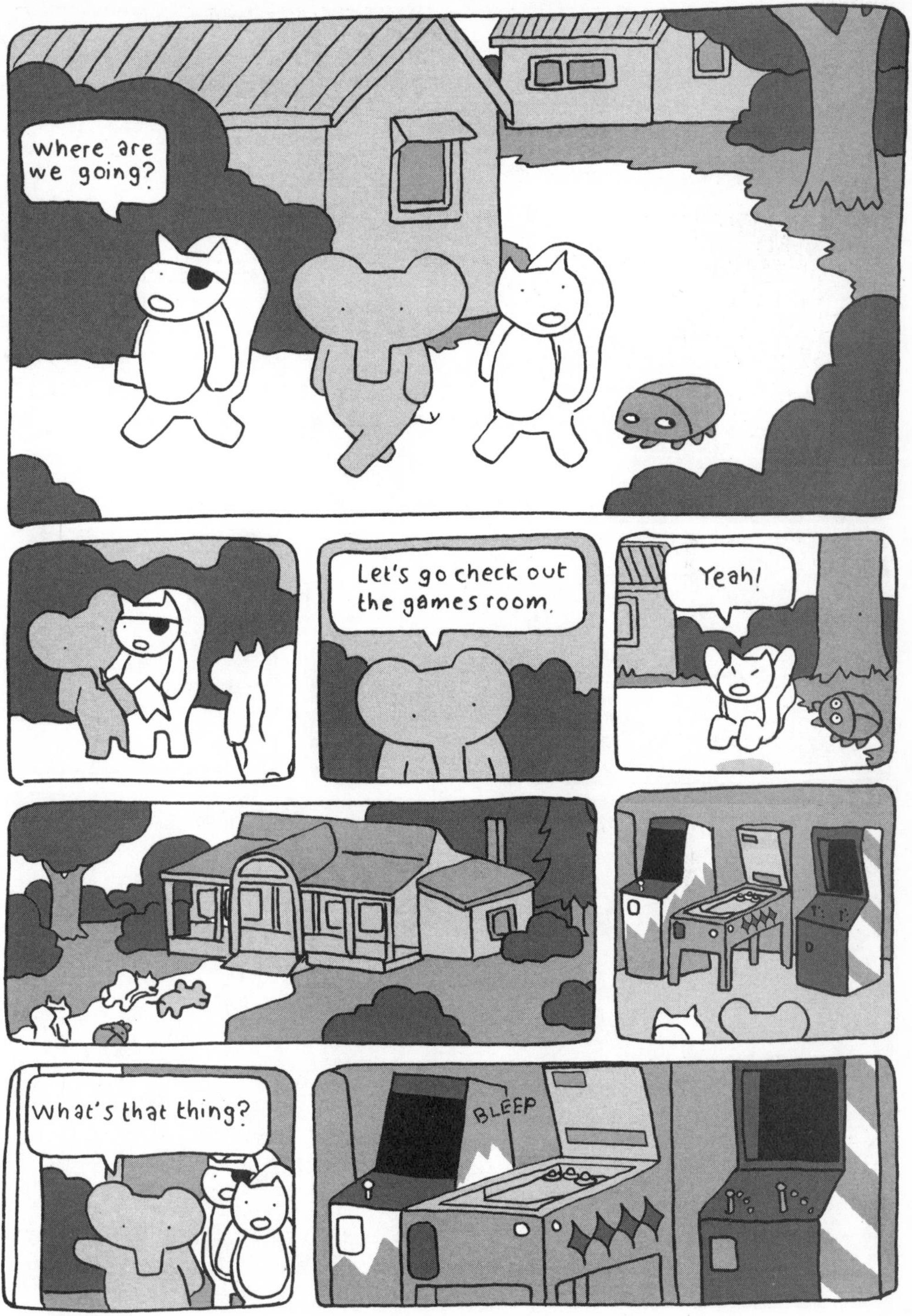

where are we going?

Bleep
Ding ding
I'm going to see the big tree.
okay.
Duckboard Forest

My turn!
My turn!

Hey, guys.

Have you seen Eden?

Um, no. She left.

I think she went to see the Admiral.

He means the General.

?

Wow!

TWEEEEEEEE

TWEEEEEEEE

What's that sound?

It's coming from up there.
TWEEEE
E

What is it?

TWEEEEEEEE

It's a beetle!

TWEEEEEE

It must be stuck.

I'll have to save it!

TWEEEEEEEEEEEE
TWEEEEEEEE
Hang on!
Sniff
EDEN!
EDEN, ARE YOU OKAY?
Hi, Mums. I'm fine.
Come down this instant.

I'll be right there.

I'm rescuing a beetle.

What!? Come down, it's dangerous.

TWEEEEEEEEEE

Aaah!

Anders!

Can you fly up and rescue Eden?

Sure can.

HOP
SKIP

Wait.

Eden knows what she's doing.

Let her try.

Hello there.

You look stuck.

TWEEEEEEEEE

Hang on, I'll help you.

Hnnn

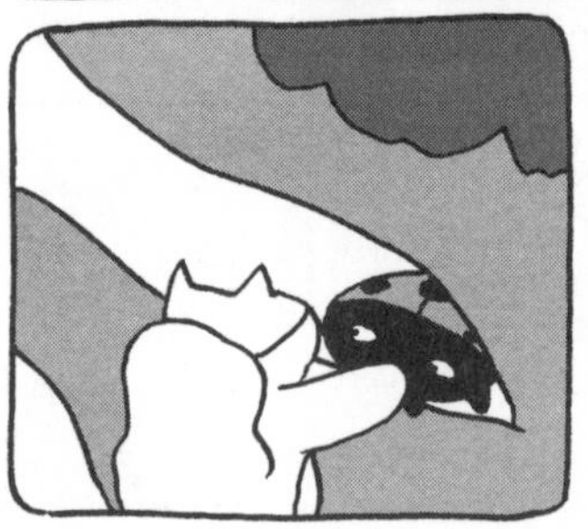

POP

Hey!

Ha ha, are you okay back there?

We're coming down now!

Be careful!

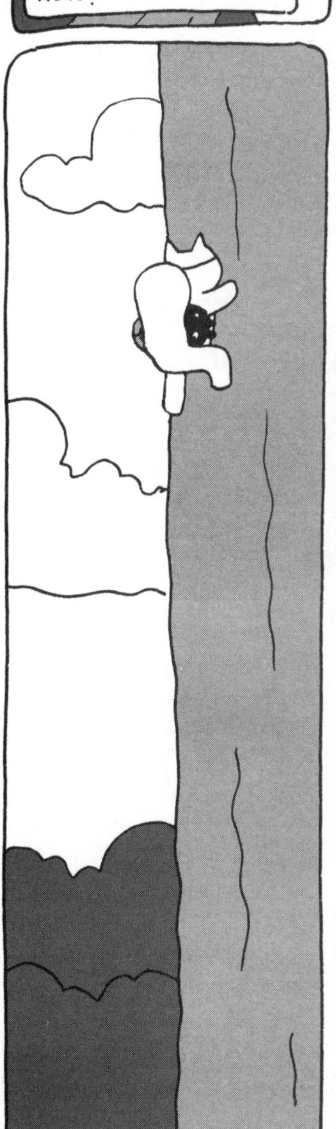

Almost there.

Eden!

Are you hurt?

No, I'm fine.

This little beetle was stuck in the tree.

Well, we're very proud of you. Let's head back to camp.
Good idea. I'm tired.
You're so brave, Eden.
Sniff sniff
HISSS
HISSS
SKIP!
Hey, cut it out, you two!
Let's go home.
Come on.
That tree is cool.

Chapter 7

ILIAD
Hey, guys.
Hi, Eden.
Let's do some Whump!
YEAH!

BYAH!
HYUH!
FWA!

HYUH!

FWA!

BYA!

Hey look, it's Veronica, the kid who can fly too.

Hi.

Hello.
Nice to meet you.

What are you guys doing?

Whump!
It's a partial art.
He means 'martial art.'

Oh, is it fighting?

No, it's thinking and moving.

Can I join in?

Sure, just copy us.

You're good at this, Veronica.
Thanks.

Later.
Volcano Information session.
Hello, everyone. I'm Ranger Nelson.
Today we are going to learn about Mount Tremble.
Mount Tremble is an extinct conical volcano, which formed over one hundred thousand years ago.
Mount Tremble is considered extinct but is known to, now and then, emit gas and clouds. Its last vent was over two hundred years ago.
Camp Canvas is located on the banks of a lake formed by the eruption of Mount Tremble, over fifty thousand years ago.

So, they're the basics about the volcano.

Any questions?

Yes?

Is the volcano going to erupt again?

No, it's not going to.

It's possible it might vent more clouds and gas. But it won't erupt with any force.

Sniff Sniff

GRRRR

Hey!

C'mere.

Come here, Skip.

Let's go outside.

I hope these guys will start to behave.

Are you going to be good, Bounce?

Hey, we should go flying together.

Sure, let's go.

That was a great talk.

Yes, it was very educational.

What's your beetle's name?

Um.

Well, she looks a bit like watermelon, so...

...Melon.

Ha ha ha ha.

C'mon, let's go play!

Hey Bernie, catch!

Catch!

Wow, Melon can fly too.

Catch, Melon!

Ha ha.

Catch!

Good one Melon.

Catch!

BRING BRING
?

Hello?

Hi Dad, it's Bernie.

Hi Bernie, how's camp?

It's okay, Dad.

Oh, that's great to hear.

Are you having fun with your friends?

I sure am.

I miss you, son.

BOO HOO

Hey Bernie, it's okay.

Listen, you know what?

What?

You are the best kid a dad could ever have. I'm so proud of you and everything you do. I'm so happy you can call me when you are sad and I can help you.

Yeah, that did help.

I love you, son. Have fun at camp.

I love you, too. Bye, Dad.

Hi, Bernie.

Are you going to hang out with us oldies?

Okay.

Chapter 8

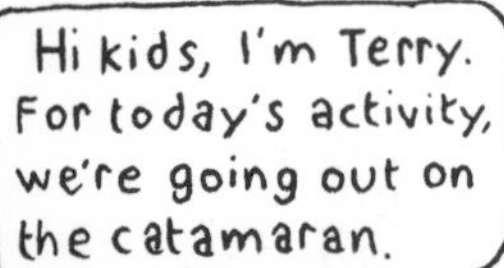
Hi kids, I'm Terry. For today's activity, we're going out on the catamaran.

What's a catamaran?

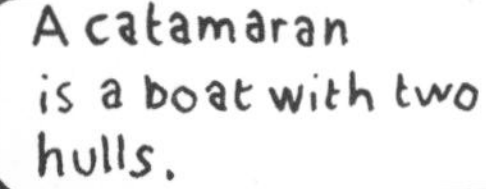
A catamaran is a boat with two hulls.

The hulls are joined together in the middle and a mast is right in the centre. It's powered by a sail, and we can steer it with the rudders.

What's your beetle's name again?

Bounce.

Why Bounce?

Because she can bounce really high. Sometimes when Bounce has a burst of speed it makes a big shock wave.

Bounce is awesome.

Hold on! It's getting choppy!

Ha ha ha ha.

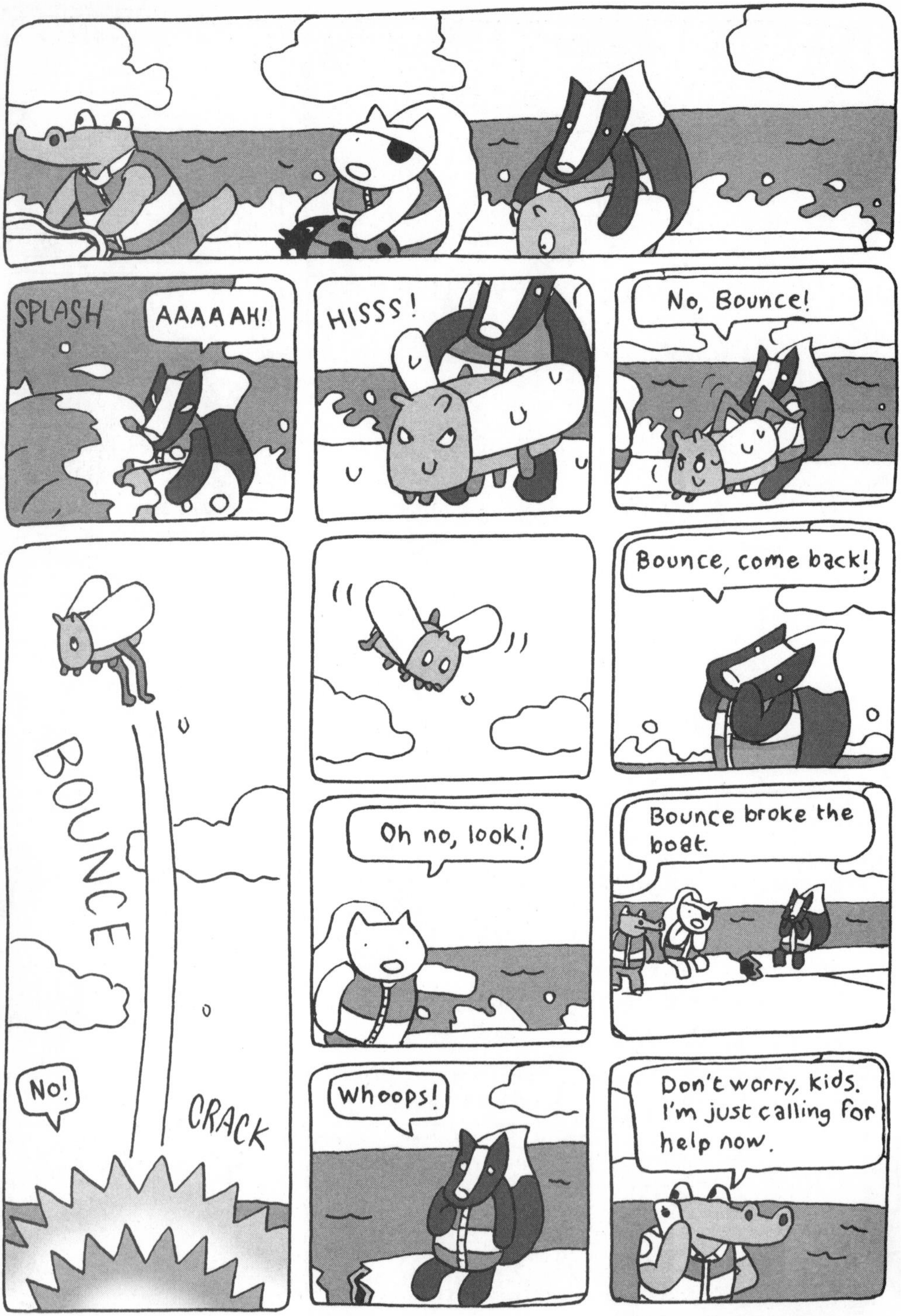

SPLASH
AAAAAH!
HISSS!
No, Bounce!

Bounce, come back!

Can we go home right now, please?
Okay.
C'mon, Skip.
Let's go.

Thanks, Skip.
Yeah, thanks Skip.
Are you okay, Bernie?
Yes. I'm just going for a walk now.
Okay.

Woah!
RUMBLE
AAAH!
!
Oh no!

WHUMP!
PUFF

Hello?
Hey, wait!
Look.

?

Hey, guys!
!
!

Wow, who's that?

This is my new beetle friend!

What's his name?
Um.
I thought he was a lump of rock, so...
...Lump!
Cool, we've all got beetle friends now.
Can Lump fly?
He has wings.
He might fly.
He can make smoke clouds, too.
Maybe we can teach him to fly.
Okay.
If he wants to.

Soon.
C'mon, Melon. Catch!
See, Lump? Melon can fly.
Your turn!
Catch!
MUNCH
LUMP!
I don't think he's ready to fly yet.

Eden, do you think you can fly with Melon?

HOP

HOP

C'mon.

Flip

Skip

Bye.
So, Lump...
...do you think you want to fly, too?
CHUNK
Woah!
CLICK
No? Okay then.

Chapter 9

What should we do today?

Let's play with the beetles!

Okay. I think Melon and I will get some flying practice in.

Lump and I can go sailing.

Cool. Want to go racing, Veronica?

Hey, yeah!

Soon.
Having fun, Lump?
This place is pretty great.
I'm glad I came here and met you, Lump.
Ha ha ha ha.

Nearby.
This is so much fun!
Ha ha ha!
Let's land over there.
Hey, not that way!
Melon!
Where are you taking me?
Stop!
Huh?!

It's an old fire watchtower.
It looks disused.
Wow.
Look, Melon!
KRUMBLZ
An old biscuit tin.
I wonder what's inside.
No biscuits.
It's full of messages.
Letters from people who've been here before.
Some of these are from years ago.
I should write one, too.

Meanwhile.
Do you want to see who's the fastest, Anders?
Okay!
Let's go!
BOUNCE
!
Hey!
BZZZZZ

Hey, that wasn't fair.
Yes it was.
I'm the fastest.
Let's have a proper race, with no powers allowed.
Pfft!
Okay then.
Let's fly to the General and back again. First one back is the fastest.
Are you ready?
I'm ready!

READY.
SET.
GO!

Ha ha, it looks like we both won!
Yeah, I guess so.
We can both be the fastest.
Let's go find Eden.
Good idea.
Look, Melon. It's Anders and Veronica.
Let's catch up!

Hi, guys.
Hi, Eden!
We were just looking for you.
I don't know about you, but I'm pretty tired.
Want to go find Bernie?
Yeah, okay.

Hi, Bernie!
what've you been up to?
oh, you know, hanging out with Lump.
Well, do you want to play with us now?
Yeah!
C'mon!

Chapter 10

The next day.

ZZZZZZZ

We should go on an adventure.

Yeah!

Where to?

Let's look at the map together.

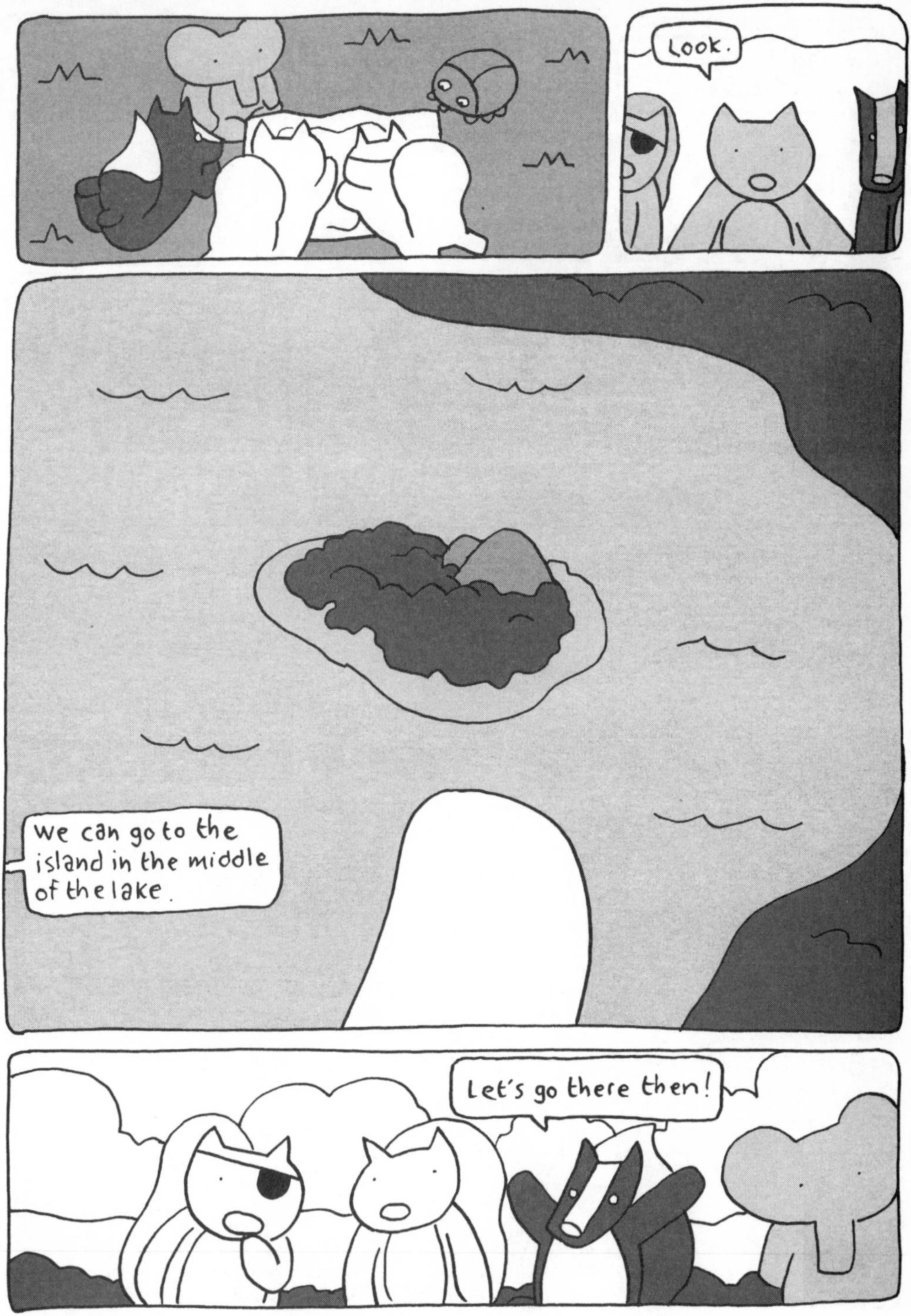

Look.

We can go to the island in the middle of the lake.

What if we go there and have a picnic?

Hey, yeah!

Great, we can take the beetles.

Wait, Lump can't fly there, though.

That won't matter.

You guys can swim over.

We'll fly there and meet up with you.

Alright, cool!

You guys get ready. I'll tell the parents.

Soon.

Have a safe trip, kids. We'll see you this afternoon.
Be back by four, okay?

Okay...
We'll be back by then.

See you there, guys!

Bye, Bernie! See you in a little while.

Alright, let's go.

Let's wait here for Bernie.

I might look around for a while.

Veronica!

Here he is!

Hello!

How was the trip?

Smooth and relaxing.

Hey guys, come quick!

I found something.

What is it?

It looks abandoned.

Let's go check it out.

Hello?

It must have been some kind of research station.
It looks like they were researching the volcano.
Well, they're gone now.
I wonder what they learned.
I don't know, but they left in a hurry.
Let's keep exploring.
Then we can come back and have our picnic.
Can you hear something?
It sounds like running water.

It's a creek!

On an island?
Where does it go?

Lump and I can go find out.

You guys can follow along on the bank.

Stop if you find something.

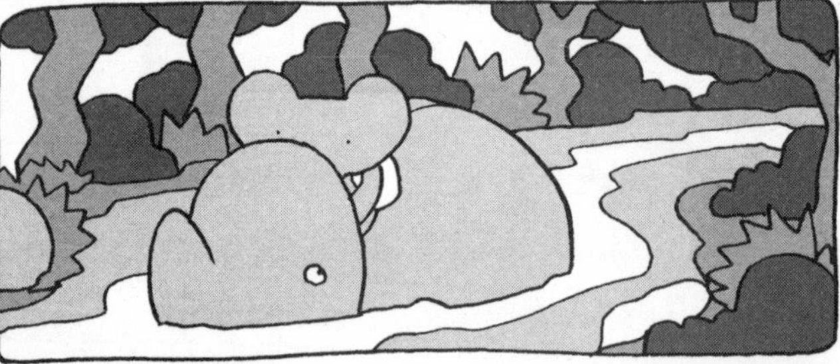

Do you think Lump could fly?
He has wings.

I don't know. He likes swimming.

All beetles can fly.

They just have to want to.

Where did Bernie go?

HEY, BERNIE!

TWEEEEEEEEEE
Bernie!
Bernie!

Look!

The creek just stops!

It just disappears.

And Bernie's disappeared too.

BERNIE!
LUMP!

Where are they?

Chapter 11

I wonder how the kids are going.

I'm sure they're fine.

Bernie! Where are you?

Bernie!
TWEEEEEEE

Down here!

Where did that come from?

This way!

Hello!

It's an underground waterfall.
Are you okay?
Yeah, we're fine.
There's a big tunnel down here.

Bernie can't fly up.

So we're going to have to go down.

Okay, let's go.

WOOOOOOOO!
WHAAAAAA!
YEEEEAAAAAHHH!

Ha ha! That was fun!
Are you sure you're okay, Bernie?
Yeah.
We were just swimming along and then we fell down the waterfall.
What is this place, Eden?
It looks to be a tunnel network.
Well, Lump can't fly, so...
...we'll have to wander this way.
Maybe there's another way out.

Hmm, there isn't a way out yet.

There may be one up ahead.

If we don't find one soon, I'll fly back for help.

HISSSS

what?

?

When a flow of lava forms a channel, the walls can build up and harden.

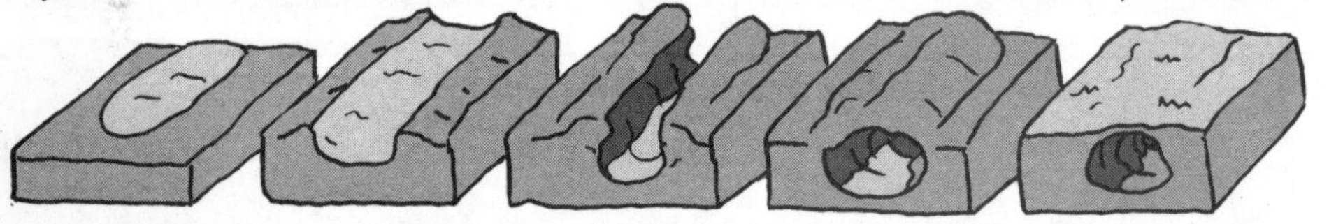

This wall can get bigger and form a tunnel over the channel.

Years later, the tunnel can collapse and open to the sky.

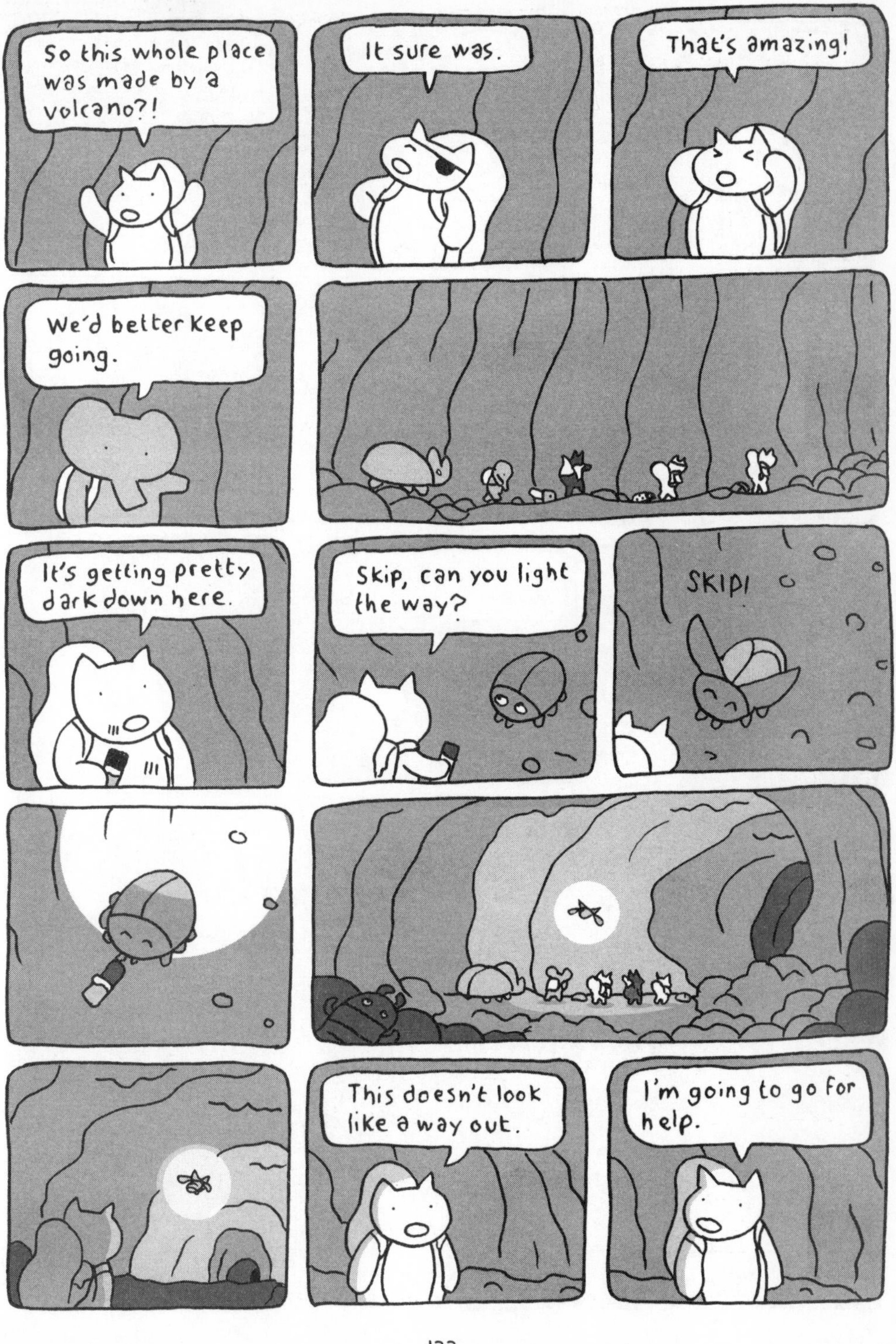

So this whole place was made by a volcano?!

It sure was.

We'd better keep going.

It's getting pretty dark down here.

Skip, can you light the way?

SKIP!

Good idea. You fly, and we'll head back to the waterfall on foot.
Can we come too?
HISSSSSSS

Cool.
HOP

We'll be back soon.

If you want to.
Sniff
Sniff

Bounce, what's wrong?

GRRRRRR

AAAAHHH!

WHUMP!!
TWEEEEEEEEEE
TWEEEEE
PUFF
TWEEEEE
TWEEEEE
TWEE
Bounce!
EEEEEE
ZIP
It's running away!
RUMBLE
CRACK

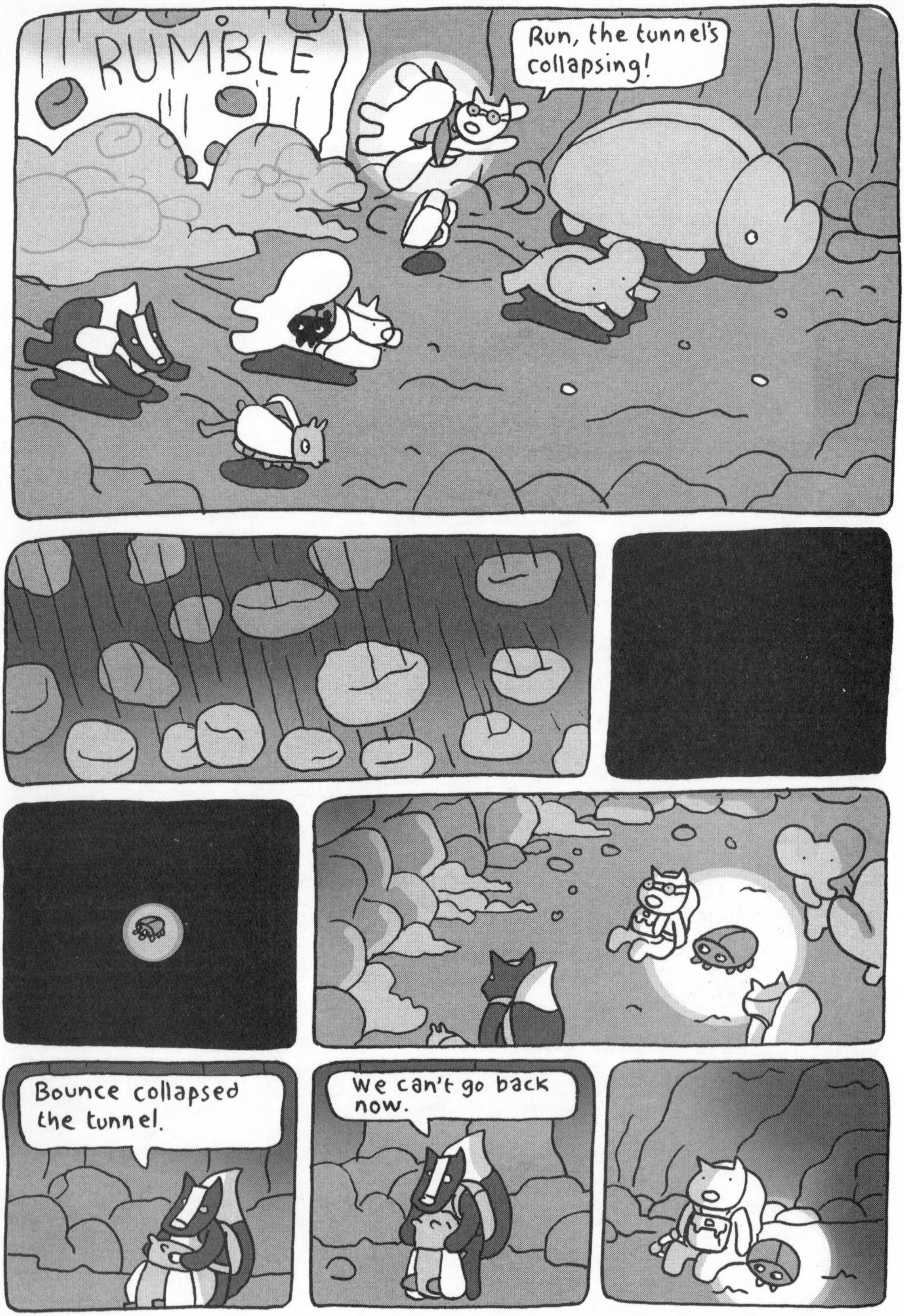

RUMBLE

Run, the tunnel's collapsing!

Chapter 12

The tunnel's blocked.

We're going to have to keep going that way.

Let's eat first, so we have energy.

Oh no, I lost my bag!

It's okay, we've got some food.

Okay, then. We'd better get going.

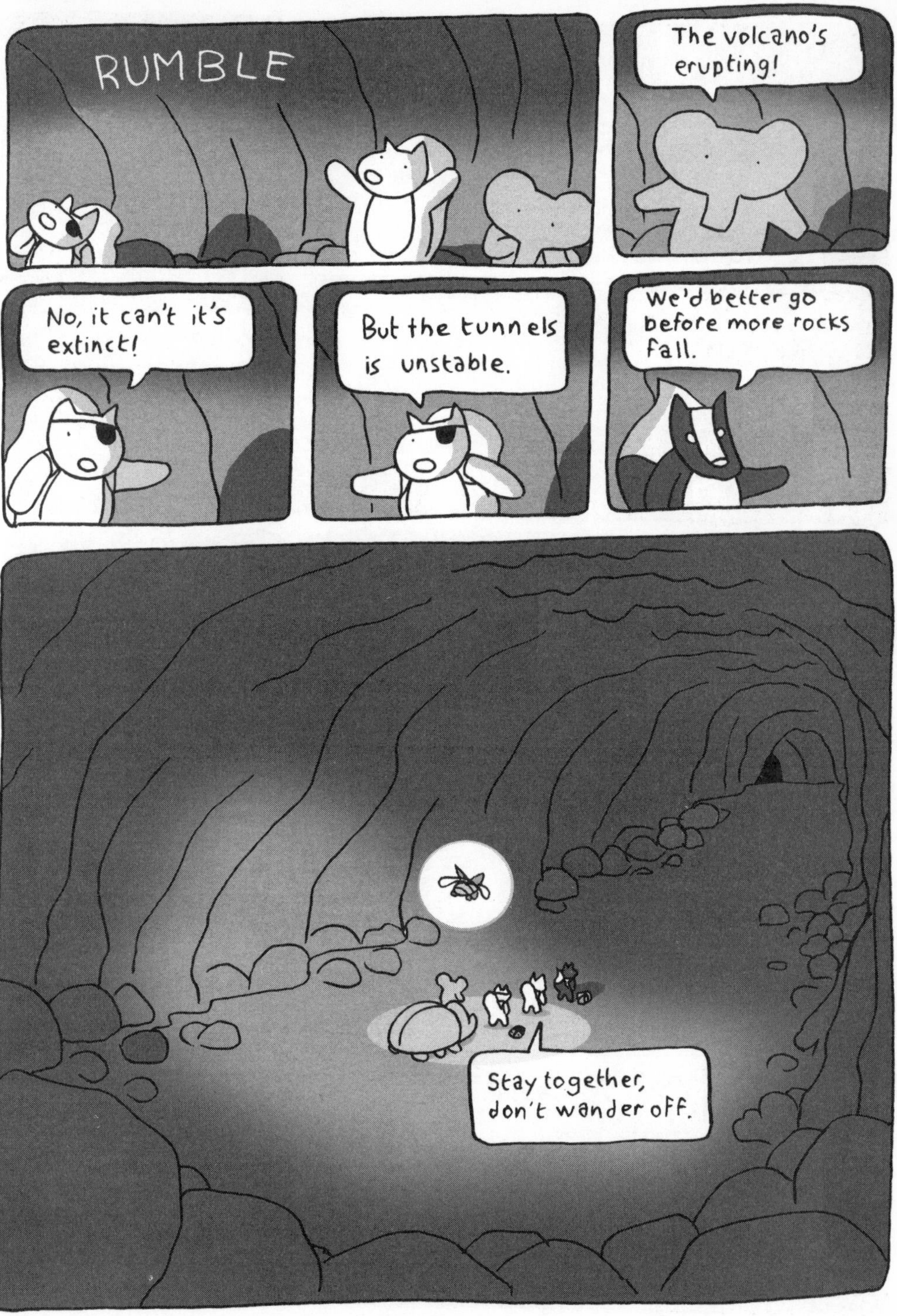

Stay together, don't wander off.

This might be scary, mightn't it?

Don't worry, Bernie. We'll be fine.

It's okay to be scared.

Skip will light the way.

It's getting warmer.

We must be near the surface.

There's a light up ahead.

C'mon!
Up here!

What is it?

We're at the bottom
of the volcano!

I can see the sky!
It's a way out!
Wow! We're right inside the volcano!
Alright, everyone.
We're going to have to fly out.

Lump, can you fly?

RUMBLE

PUFF

It's okay, Lump.

It's fine.

Melon, get ready!

C'mon, Bounce.

RUMBLE

Bounce, stay calm!
I'm not ready!

No!
BOUNCE

Veronica!

CRACK
CRACK

Oh no!

The ground is cracking.

More rocks are going to fall!

What do we do? What do we do?
TWEE
EE

HOP

Lump?

Bernie needs your help.

Meanwhile.

Is there meant to be smoke coming from the volcano?

The extinct volcano?

Lump?
I've always wanted to be brave...
...and do something amazing.
I know you're afraid. So am I.
But this is our chance.
We get to be brave now.
SKIP
Hyah!
Let's go, Lump!
CHUNK

BUZZZZZ
The rocks are falling! They're filling in the cracks!
Let's get out of here!

There they are!

Anders!

Are you guys okay?
Yes, Mum!
Is the volcano erupting?
No, it's extinct!
I'm so sorry, I went to get help.
That's okay, we are all safe now!

Chapter 13

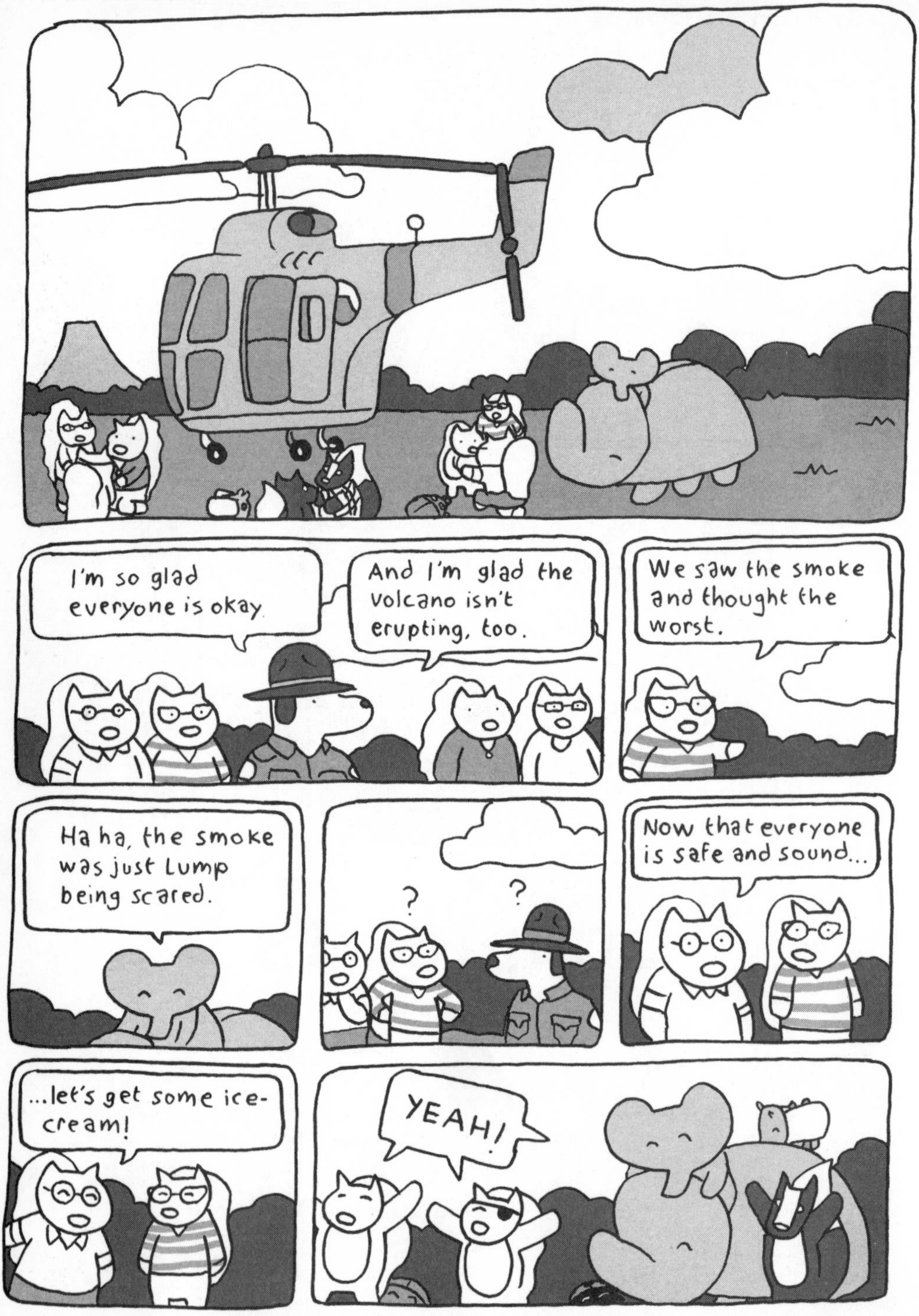

Ha ha, the smoke was just Lump being scared.

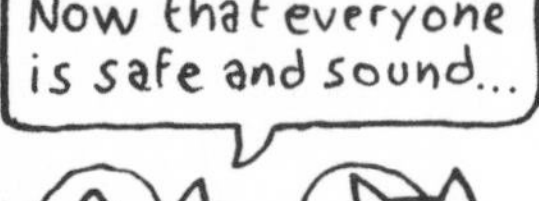

The next day.

This is the best holiday ever.

Thanks for inviting me, Anders.

That's okay, Bernie.

Hey guys, it's time to start packing up. We have to drive home soon.

Awwwww, Mum.

Come on, Anders. It's time to go.

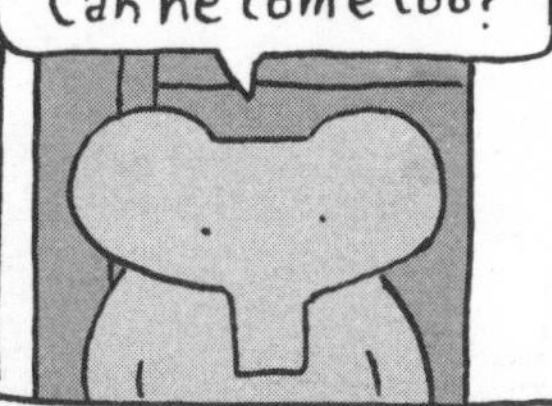
What about Lump? Can he come too?

Yes. I was going to tell you about that.

Honk honk
Dad!
Hi, Bernie!
Dad, what are you doing here?
I heard you have a new friend.
So I drove over to pick you guys up.
Thanks, Dad.
This is Lump.
Well, I'm pleased to meet you, Lump.
CHUNK
Ha ha ha ha.

Then.

Hello there.

Oh hi, Veronica.

We're off home now, too.

It's been fun hanging out.

Hi, Veronica. Are you going now?

Yes, we're leaving in a few minutes.

It's been great to meet you!

Let's catch up back in Rumple!

That's a great idea. We can all go flying.

Yeah, maybe.

See ya.
Bye.

Bye, guys. We're off now.

Okay, bye.
See ya!

Well, see you at home, Anders.

How will you get Lump home?

Well...

...come and see.

Ha ha ha.

Are you cosy, Lump?

Chunk

Bye, Anders. See you soon.

Honk honk

It's time to go, Anders.
I know.

The next day.
How's the diorama going, Anders?
Good!
I'm making a model of a volcano.
Watch.
Ha ha ha ha.

TWEEEEEEEEEE
?
That sounds like Melon!
Can I go and play, Dad?
Sure can!
C'mon, Skip!
SKIP

Hey, guys!
Hi, Anders!
Let's go!

How do volcanoes form?
The Earth is full of melted rocks, called lava.
Lava can leak through the Earth's surface.
As the lava cools it turns back into rock.
The rock can build up...
... and form a volcano!
Volcanoes are sometimes millions of years old, and many are active today!

Dear Visitor,

I found this place by accident, after my beetle, Melon, led me here.

I think that it's quite wonderful that this place exists and people choose to leave messages for other visitors who chance upon it.

You can see the whole Mt Tremble area from here, and I am reminded of the beauty of nature and the mystery of the volcano.

I hope you find a beetle too, so you can see this magical place from the skies.

Eden

Acknowledgements

Thanks to Rohan, Lucas, Charlotte, Harvey and Nora. I would also like to thank Erica Wagner, Elise Jones and Sandra Nobes for their support, patience and skill. Thanks, too, to Meg Whelan, Anna Fabris and Hilary Reynolds. Special thanks to Charlotte Watson.

About the Author

Gregory Mackay has been making comics since school. He enjoys drawing and watercolour painting. He likes drawing aeroplanes and machines, as well as building models and painting pictures. *Anders and the Comet* was his first book for children.

Have you read Anders' first adventure?

Stay tuned for Anders'
next adventure!

ANDERS
and the
CASTLE

Gregory Mackay